How Earth's Surface Change?

HOUGHTON MIFFLIN HARCOURT

PHOTOGRAPHY CREDITS: COVER ©Daniel Grill/Alamy Images; 4 (b) Image Ideas/Jupiterimages/Getty Images; 5 (t) ©Robert Glusic/Spirit/Corbis; 6 (t) ©Digital Vision/Getty Images; (b) ©Westend61/Getty Images; 9 (t) ©Photodisc/Getty Images; 10 (b) ©Houghton Mifflin Harcourt; 12 (b) ©Buena Vista Images/Getty Images; 13 (t) ©Steven Roberts/National Center for Atmospheric Research; 14 (r) ©Hola Images/Getty Images; 15 (b) ©Daniel Grill/Alamy Images; 16 (t) ©Joanne Harris and Daniel Bubnich/Shutterstock; 16 (t) ©Corbis; 17 (b) Robert Glusic/Corbis; 17 ©InterNetwork Media/Getty Images

Copyright © by Houghton Mifflin Harcourt Publishing Company

All rights reserved. No part of this work may be reproduced or transmitted in any form or by any means, electronic or mechanical, including photocopying or recording, or by any information storage and retrieval system, without the prior written permission of the copyright owner unless such copying is expressly permitted by federal copyright law. Requests for permission to make copies of any part of the work should be addressed to Houghton Mifflin Harcourt Publishing Company, Attn: Contracts, Copyrights, and Licensing, 9400 Southpark Center Loop, Orlando, Florida 32819-8647.

If you have received these materials as examination copies free of charge, Houghton Mifflin Harcourt Publishing Company retains title to the materials and they may not be resold. Resale of examination copies is strictly prohibited.

Possession of this publication in print format does not entitle users to convert this publication, or any portion of it, into electronic format.

Printed in U.S.A.

ISBN: 978-0-544-07273-2

3 4 5 6 7 8 9 10 1083 21 20 19 18 17 16 15 14

4500470073   A B C D E F G

Be an Active Reader!

Look for each word in yellow along with its meaning.

landform	plain	flood
mountain	plateau	weathering
valley	volcano	erosion
canyon	earthquake	glacier

Underlined sentences answer these questions.

What is a landform?
What are some different landforms?
How do volcanoes change Earth's crust?
How do earthquakes change Earth's crust?
What happens during a flood?
What happens during a landslide?
What can change the shape of a rock?
How does erosion change Earth's surface?
How does a glacier change Earth's surface?

What is a landform?

Imagine you are flying high in a balloon. You look down at the ground. You see that the land does not look the same everywhere. In different places the land has different shapes.

A <mark>landform</mark> is a part of Earth's surface. It has a special shape. A landform is created naturally.

Landforms include mountains, hills, valleys, plains, and canyons.

What are some different landforms?

Mountains, hills, valleys, canyons, plains, and plateaus are all landforms.

A hill is higher than the land around it. A hill is rounded at the top.

A mountain is a landform that is much higher than the surrounding land. It has sides that slope toward the top.

Guadalupe Peak is much taller than the land around it.

Plains are perfect for growing crops such as wheat.

A valley is the low land between mountains or hills. A canyon is a special kind of valley. It has very steep sides. A plain is a large flat landform. It spreads over a wide area. A plateau is a large flat landform, too. It is like a plain, but is higher than the area around it.

How do volcanoes change Earth's crust?

Volcanoes have different shapes.

Landforms come from changes in Earth's surface. Some of these changes happen quickly. Some happen slowly.

Volcanoes can change the surface quickly. A volcano is a mountain made by melted rock. The melted rock flows through an opening in Earth's crust. The crust is the outer layer of Earth.

What makes this happen? Sometimes it starts when two pieces of Earth's crust move. This can cause rocks to melt. Melted rock can come up through cracks and on to the land. When the melted rock hardens, it makes the sides of the volcano. It can also plug up the opening.

If the cooled lava plugs up the opening, more lava can't get out. Pressure builds up. If the pressure gets high enough, the new lava can break through the plug. This is an eruption. Eruptions can be very powerful. They can make big changes on Earth.

As the lava cools, it can plug the volcano. New lava can break through. It can cause an eruption.

How do earthquakes change Earth's crust?

An earthquake is a shaking of Earth's surface. It can cause land to rise and fall. Do you remember that moving pieces of Earth's crust can cause volcanoes? They can also cause earthquakes.

The pieces push and slide against each other. When the pieces stick, tension builds. When the pieces slide, they release lots of energy. This energy can make the ground shake and the surface rise or fall.

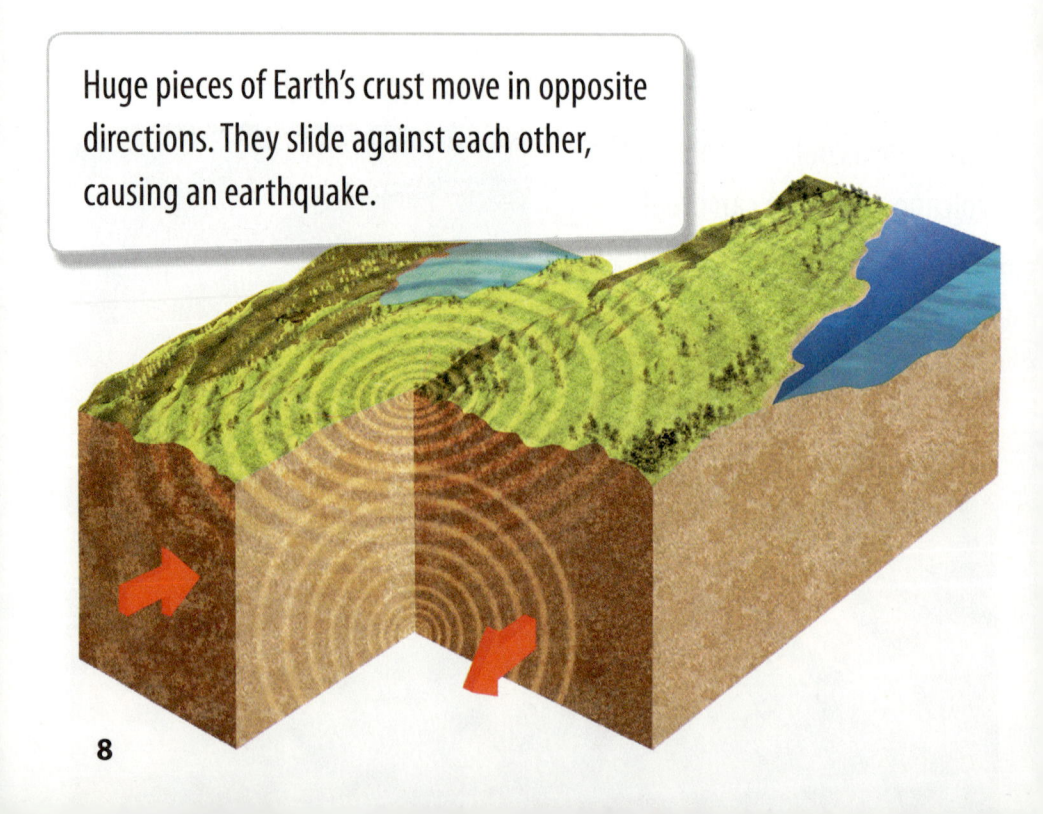

Huge pieces of Earth's crust move in opposite directions. They slide against each other, causing an earthquake.

Strong earthquakes can quickly make big changes in Earth's surface.

Most earthquakes are too weak to be felt. However, strong earthquakes can cause big changes in Earth's surface. They can cause Earth to bend, crack open, or move to a new position.

Strong earthquakes can hurt people and damage property. Earthquakes under the sea can cause giant waves called tsunamis.

What happens during a flood?

A flood can also bring a quick change to Earth's surface. A flood is an overflow of water from a river, stream, lake, or sea. This happens when rivers, streams, or lakes become too full. Heavy rain can cause an overflow. So can rain that lasts a long time. Storm winds can blow seawater onto shore.

A flood moves water onto dry land. It can also move rocks, soil, and debris. These changes can harm some plants and animals. For example, if a tree's roots are underwater for too long, the tree can drown. These changes sometimes help plants and animals. A flood can bring plants water and make the soil richer.

The floodwaters move rocks and soil. They can move trees and fill buildings, too.

Floodwater can damage things by getting them wet. An example is a carpet in a basement. But floodwater can also damage things by bumping into them. A lot of water moving fast can knock down trees and damage buildings.

After some time, the water from a flood goes away. The water can soak into the ground and dry up. Or it can flow back into a river, stream, lake, or ocean.

Flood Safety Checklist

What should I do?
- ☑ Listen to area radio and television stations and a NOAA Weather Radio for possible warnings.
- ☑ Be prepared to evacuate at a moment's notice.

What supplies do I need?
- ☑ Water – at least a 3-day supply; one gallon per person per day.
- ☑ Food – at least a 3-day supply of non-perishable, easy-to-prepare food.
- ☑ Flashlight

What do I do after a flood?
- ☑ Return home only when officials have declared the area safe.
- ☑ Before entering your home, look outside for loose power lines, damaged gas lines, foundation cracks, or other damage.
- ☑ Watch out for wild animals.

It's important to be prepared if you live in an area that could be flooded.

What happens during a landslide?

During a landslide, rock and soil fall down a slope. Land moves down the slope from place to place. The landslide changes the shape of Earth's surface.

The landslide gets bigger and stronger. It might grow big enough to uproot a tree or move a house.

What causes this? Material on the slope becomes unstable and falls. The falling pieces bump into new things. This makes them fall, too.

Water from rain or a flood can soak into the soil. Wet soil is heavier than dry soil.

A landslide quickly changes Earth's surface.

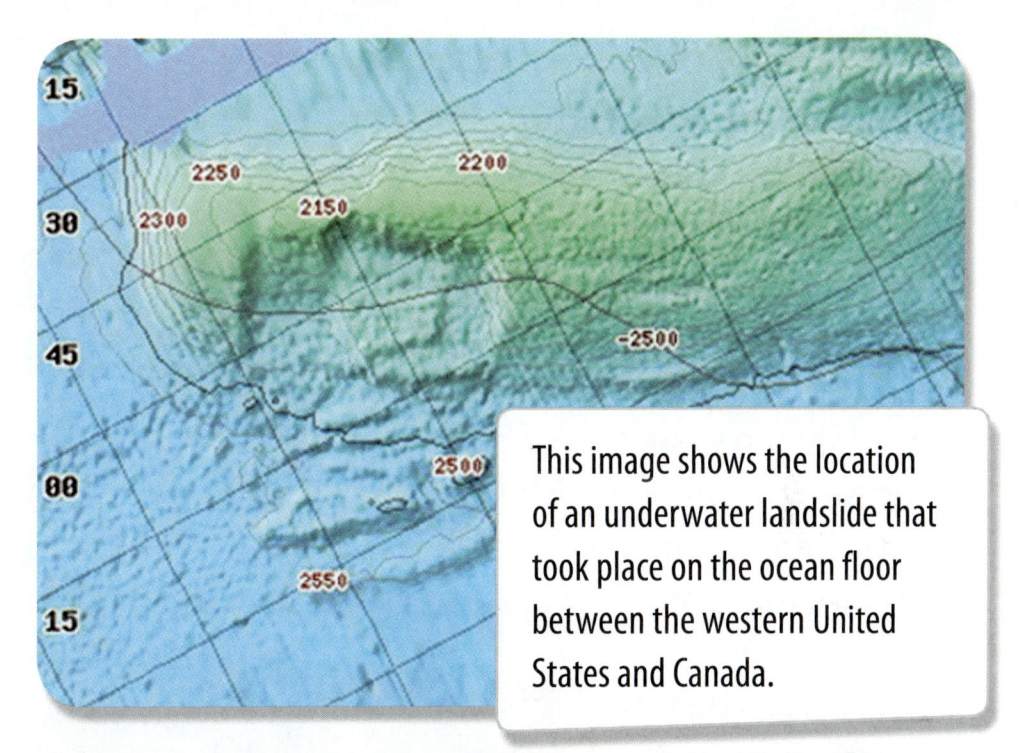

This image shows the location of an underwater landslide that took place on the ocean floor between the western United States and Canada.

If the soil gets too heavy, the slope may not be able to hold it up. The heavier soil may fall and start a landslide.

Earthquakes can start landslides too. The shaking from the earthquake can loosen soil and rocks and start them falling. This can happen under the sea, too. Sometimes landslides under the sea cause tsunamis.

Even volcanoes can cause landslides. The ash and debris can build up. They can make the soil and rock on the slope heavy enough to slide down.

What can change the shape of a rock?

Not all changes to Earth's surface are quick. ==Weathering== is a slow change. Weathering happens when natural forces change the shape of rock. Wind and water can do this. Over many years they can wear stone away.

Weathering can also crack rock and break it into pieces. Tree roots can do this. They can grow under rock and break it into pieces.

Water can do this. It can get into cracks in a rock. When the water freezes, it gets bigger. This makes the crack bigger. The rock begins to crumble.

These tree roots grew slowly into the rock. Over time, the roots broke the rock apart.

14

Water can break down rock. Waves slam into the rock over and over. This breaks the rock into smaller pieces.

Wind can lift sand and slam it into rock. The sand breaks off pieces of the rock.

What happens to this broken rock? The rock can turn into sand or mix with plant and animal remains to make soil.

Flowing water smoothed and shaped these rocks.

Wave Rock, Western Australia

You can guess why this 15-meter weathered granite surface is called Wave Rock!

How does erosion change Earth's surface?

Weathering breaks rock into smaller pieces, such as sand. Erosion moves gravel, sand, and soil on Earth's surface from one place to another. Erosion can change Earth's surface greatly.

Water and wind cause erosion. Rain washes soil away. Rivers and streams carry sand downstream. Wind blows sand and soil from a field or mountain.

Gravity helps cause erosion. Gravity pulls things downward. It helps wind and water move rock and soil to a new place. It helps them change Earth's surface.

How does a glacier change Earth's surface?

A glacier is a large, thick sheet of ice. Some glaciers grow, some melt and shrink. Some stay the same size. The ice in glaciers moves very slowly downhill.

As glacier ice moves, it can cut paths in the ground. Glaciers can pick up rock and soil and carry them to a different place. In these ways glaciers can change the shape of Earth's surface.

glacier

A glacier is a thick sheet of ice. It can change Earth's surface. It can push land aside or carry it to someplace new.

Responding

Create a Model

Use a piece of cardboard as a base. Then use clay to create a model of the following landforms: mountain, valley, canyon, plain, and plateau. Label each landform. Use the glossary to review what makes each landform different.

Describe a Process

Choose a natural event you learned about in this unit. In a paragraph, describe what happens before, during, and after the event. In your "After" section, explain how the event could change Earth's surface.

Glossary

canyon [KAN·yuhn] A valley with steep sides. *The canyon had very steep sides.*

earthquake [ERTH·kwayk] A shaking of Earth's surface that can cause land to rise and fall. *The earth shook during the earthquake.*

erosion [i·ROH·zhuhn] The process of moving weathered rock and soil from one place to another. *Erosion moves rock and soil to new places.*

flood [FLUHD] A large amount of water that covers normally dry land. *The water from the flood covered the field.*

glacier [GLAY·sher] A large, thick sheet of slow-moving ice. *The glacier cut a valley in the mountainside.*

landform [LAND·fawrm] A natural shape or feature on Earth's surface. *We saw several landforms, such as mountains and valleys.*

mountain [MOUNT·uhn] The highest kind of land, with sides that slope toward its top. *The mountain had very tall sides.*

plain [PLAYN] Flat land that spreads out a long way. *We could see for miles across the flat plain.*

plateau [pla·TOH] A flat area higher than the land around it. *The flat plateau was higher than the land around it.*

valley [VAL·ee] The low land between mountains or hills. *There was a valley between the two hills.*

volcano [vahl·KAY·noh] A mountain made of lava, ash, or other materials from eruptions. *From a distance, the volcano looked like a mountain.*

weathering [WETH·er·ing] The breaking down of rocks on Earth's surface into smaller pieces. *Weathering broke the rock into smaller pieces.*